*This book was made especially for:*

# MASON

Dear Mason,

Words cannot express how special you are.
But, here are twenty-six that try! Each one so
perfectly describes you. You are all of these
wonderful qualities— and so much more.

Love,

A is for *amazing.*
That's Mason
in every way!

# B

is for the special way you *brighten* up each day.

**C** is for your *courage.*
You don't fear
what to do.

# D

is for your *daring*.
You always
carry through.

# E

is for your *energy*,
so vibrant and
so bright!

**F** is for the *fun* you bring to all both day and night.

G describes your future. Oh, the places you will *go!*

**H** is for the *heights* you'll climb and successes you will know.

I's *imagination* and the power of your dreams.

J is for the *joy* you bring, your shining face that beams.

# K

is for your *kindness*,
shown to big and small.

**L** is for the *love* you freely share with one and all.

**M** is for your *music*, the song of your own heart.

**N** is meant for *never*, for we'll never, *ever* part.

O means there is *one* you—there never will be two!

**P** is meant for *perfect*—it's you just being you.

Q is all the *qualities*
I notice every time.

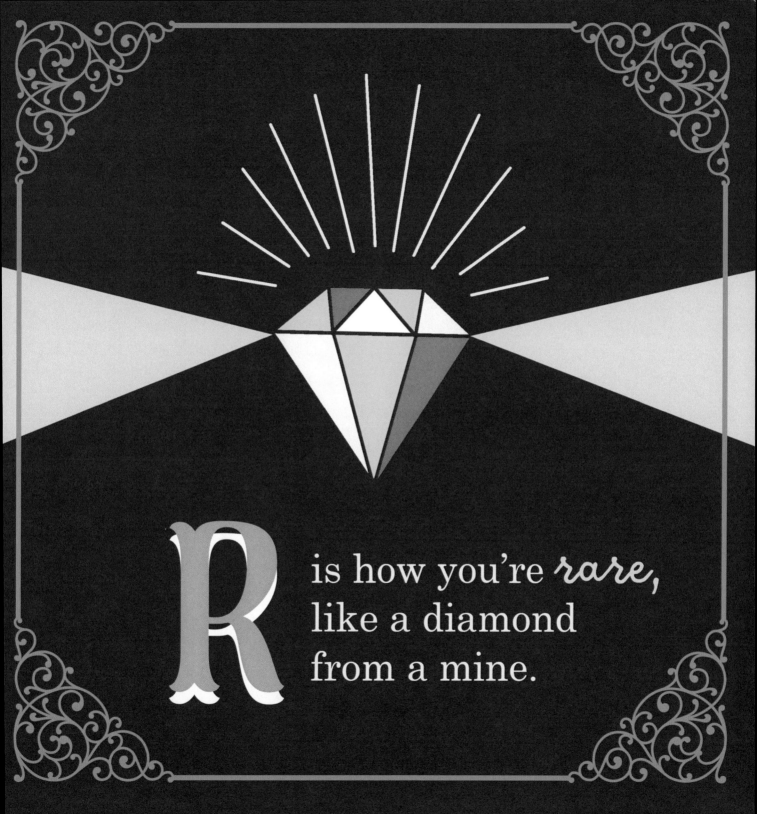

R is how you're *rare*, like a diamond from a mine.

S is meant for *super*, for you have pow'r to soar!

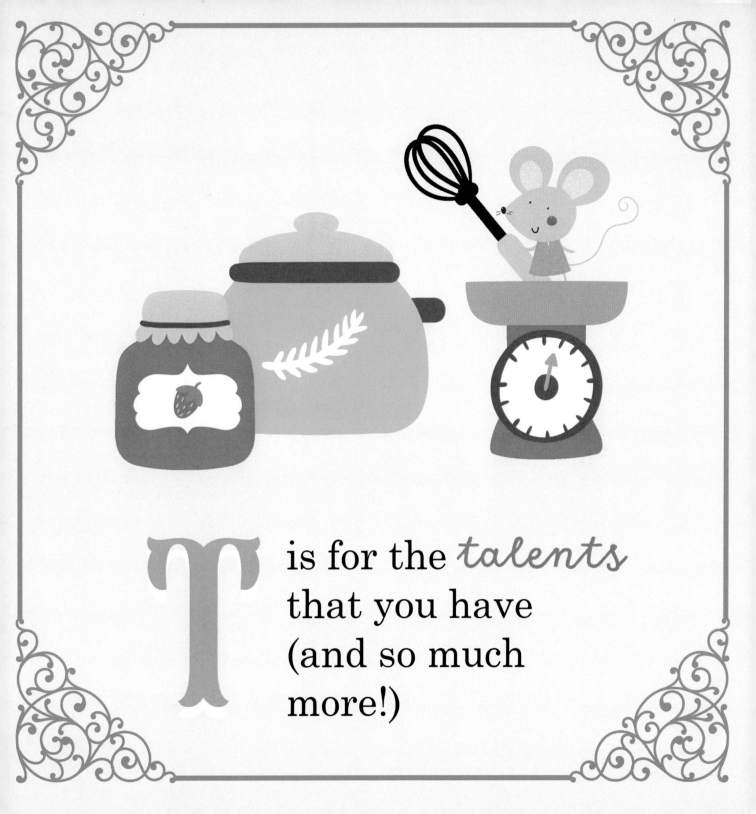

T is for the *talents* that you have (and so much more!)

U is for *unique* in every bold sense of the word.

**V** is for your *voice*.
Don't be afraid
that you'll
be heard!

**W** is for *wild*.
Always live and
gallop free!

X

is xceptional,
xtraordinarily!

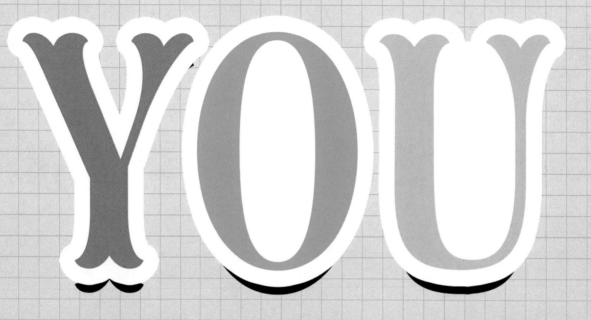

# YOU

**Y** is meant for *you*,
the only one
there'll ever be.

But day is done, and you must sleep, so

Z now stands for zzzzzzzzzzzz...

## Li'l Llama
CUSTOM KIDS BOOKS

Made in the USA
Monee, IL
20 November 2024

70670016R00019